Praying for Crows

by Lynda Eymann

Violet Hill Press

Praying for Crows

by Lynda Eymann

Published by Violet Hill Press
First Paperback Edition
January 2014

This book is a work of fiction.

All rights reserved.
No part of this book may be copied or reproduced in any printed, electronic, or audio format whatsoever without written permission from the author.

Some of the stories in this collection were previously published under the pseudonym Missy Valentine.

Copyright © 2014 by Lynda Eymann
Cover Art Copyright © 2014 by Violet Hill Press

ISBN 13: 978-0-9778186-0-0
ISBN 10: 0-9778186-0-8

Contents

Short Stories & Essays

The Most Precious Gift ~ 1
Don't Catch a Falling Star ~ 9
Mama's Gift ~12
The Ozarks ~ 32
Marooned ~ 35
Who's Afraid of the Big Bad Goats? ~ 42
The Wild October Sea ~ 48
A Time to be Born ~ 65
Brother Hop-a-long ~ 79

Haiku

Author's Note ~ 86
Spring ~ 91
Summer ~ 101
Autumn ~ 121
Winter ~ 133

Childhood Poems ~ 145

About the Author ~ 166
Books by Lynda Eymann ~ 166

For

my husband
my parents
my family

And for
the girl
I used to be

pay her no mind
she's just an old lady
that prays for crows

The Most Precious Gift

for my mother

"Everyone in the world is born with a gift," Ma said, while she knelt in the garden beside me, her back turned to the setting sun. I could feel her glance at me as she gently lifted a tomato leaf and examined its underside. Sitting cross-legged in her cool shadow, I poked the freshly hoed dirt with a stick and didn't say a word.

"Everyone is born with a gift," Ma repeated, "and that gift should never be wasted."

At eight years of age, I had heard Ma say the same thing to each of us a thousand times. It had always seemed to be true, but I was starting to wonder. Everyone in my family had a gift—except for me. My older sister, Evelyn, had a gift for singing in a voice so sweet and pure that it made you feel as if you were sitting on a cloud at the very edge of heaven. My little sister, Anna, could play the piano by ear alone, rendering any song she wished with her short, determined fingers, never missing a note. And Ma—Ma could sing just like Patsy Cline, breaking our hearts with songs about Old Shep and dying cowboys and poor wooden Indians every summer night as we sat on the front porch steps, beneath the stars and the moon and the sycamore trees. Everyone, even the crickets and whippoorwills, would fall silent to hear the strum of Ma's guitar and the sad, smooth ache of her voice as another poor cowboy hit the dust.

Pa and I had no gift for music whatsoever. That made me cry all the harder each time Old Shep or another cowboy went to heaven. I cried once for Shep—and once for the cowboy—and then I cried for myself, knowing that I sounded like a wounded bullfrog instead of our beloved Patsy Cline. Pa couldn't carry a tune either, but he had so many other gifts that it didn't seem to matter. He could milk a cow in less than 30 seconds flat, could shoot a tin can from 100 yards away, and he could beat any man anywhere in any fast and furious game of horseshoes.

Even our dog, Bootsie, had a gift. He had the ability to grab a snake—whether it was a water moccasin, a rattlesnake, or an innocent black snake—and kill it faster than Pa could reach for a hoe or a shovel. Bootsie would shake those snakes back and forth so hard that they would fly into shreds right before our eyes. And he had a gift for finding the snakes as well. They seemed to be wherever we went—in the barn, by the outhouse door, on the creek bank. One moment I would be stepping across a path. The next moment, a dead, shredded snake would be lying at my feet, and Bootsie would be standing over it, panting and wagging his tail, waiting to be praised for his gift.

"I know it's true everyone has a gift," I said to Ma, as we headed to the house, a basket of tomatoes and squash between us. "It's true for everyone, except for me. I can't sing like you and Evelyn. I can't play the piano like Anna. I can't do anything Pa can do." I tripped on a stone in the path just then. "I can't even *walk* without falling on my face."

"Everyone has a gift, Sarah," Ma said. "We just don't know what yours is yet."

I sulked through the rest of the evening, dutifully eating only two legs of Ma's fried chicken and only two helpings of mashed potatoes with gravy. I sulked as Evelyn and Anna and I did the dishes, and I cried harder than usual when Old Shep died on the front porch after supper, the stars blurring and then disappearing altogether in the clear, black sky. I was still sulking when Ma came to say good-night to us, after climbing the steep, creaking stairs to our narrow bedroom which was tucked beneath the eaves of our house.

"Do you need an extra quilt tonight, Sarah?" Ma asked me, as she opened the stiff, crooked window next to my bed. I shivered as a cool breath of mountain air entered the room.

"No, Ma," I answered, but Ma spread another quilt across me and tucked it around my shoulders, knowing that I was always cold, even on summer nights.

"Maybe I have a gift for being cold," I said, my bitterness only partially muffled by the layers of quilts.

I could hear the suppressed laughter in Ma's voice as she kissed Evelyn and Anna goodnight.

"I don't think so, Sarah," she answered, and then she left the room, leaving Evelyn and Anna to their quiet dreams and me to my dismal images of a dark future with no talent for anything.

I was still sulking the next morning as I went about my chores—hauling a bucket of water from the well to the kitchen, gathering the eggs in the chicken house, and then helping Pa and Evelyn as they fed and milked our eighteen cows. Bootsie followed me wherever I went, wagging his black and white tail, keeping his eyes on the ground, ready for any opportunity to use his special gift. Only two weeks ago, he had spotted and killed a rattlesnake that had been coiled by the barn door before it had a chance to shake its rattle.

As Pa and Evelyn were loading the truck to make their delivery to the milk plant in town, Pa stopped to pour some fresh, foaming milk into a bowl for me to give to the two stray kittens that had wandered into our barn a few days ago. The kittens were as skittish as squirrels, but Pa told me that the milk—and patience—would tame them in time.

Oh, how I longed to touch those kittens! They looked so soft and white that I had named them

Cotton and Candy. Only Ma and I could tell them apart, merely by the way they squinted their eyes when they looked up at us. I had claimed Cotton as my own cat, and I had promised the other kitten to Anna, as soon as they were tame. Anna dreamed of bringing her kitten into the house, if we could talk Ma into it. Ma had two rules by which we lived: No one should *ever* tell a lie, and animals belonged outside, in the barn, *never* in the house. We would remind her—truthfully—of all the benefits that a cat could provide in an old house so easily accessed by mice. We knew it was a long shot, but we hoped Ma would eventually agree with us. Maybe—just maybe—she would allow a cat in the house.

"Kitty kitty kitty kitty kitty kitty!!"

They didn't answer me at first, but I finally heard their soft meows coming from behind two bales of hay near the side door.

"Oh! You're down from the loft, you sweet little kitties!"

I could see their eyes in the shadows, as wide and as shiny as blue marbles. When I stepped closer, my kitten ducked down and inched backward into the dark crevice between the bales of hay, but Anna's kitten meowed plaintively and came forward, slinking close to the ground. He hesitated in front of the bowl of milk and looked up at me, trusting me, as I crouched down to see him better. My hand was hovering above his back. I could almost feel his warm, snowy-white fur beneath my fingertips. I was almost touching him—almost. But then I heard a snarl in the open doorway behind me. Before I could turn to look, Bootsie was leaping over my shoulder and grabbing the kitten by the neck and shaking him back and forth—again and again and again—while I screamed and screamed for him to stop.

A moment later, Anna's dead kitten was lying at my feet, and Bootsie was standing over him, panting and wagging his tail, waiting for the praise that always followed the killing of a snake.

Ma heard my frantic screams from the house. She came running with her hair and the strings of her apron flying behind her, a broom in one hand and a rolling pin in the other. When she saw the kitten hanging from my outstretched hands like a limp white rag, she tossed the broom and rolling pin aside and wrapped her arms around me, trying to console me as I sobbed harder and harder.

"Mama! Bootsie killed the kitty! The kitty! The kitty!" By now Bootsie knew he had done something wrong. He was cowering at my feet, cringing at every sob, begging to be punished.

Anna, who had trailed behind Ma, began to scream as soon as she saw what had happened.

"My kitty! My kitty! My kitty!" she shrieked. Even above my own sobs, I could hear her grief piercing the morning air over and over again, as she continued to scream louder and louder, unable to catch her breath. "My kitty my kitty my kitty my K-K-K-KITTY!"

I let go of Ma and put my arms around my little sister. "No, Anna," I lied. "It wasn't *your* kitty. It was *mine*. Your kitty is okay. See? He's still in the hay, right there."

Anna hiccupped and swallowed a sob as she peered into the crevice between the two bales of hay. I held my breath as she reached in and pulled out the tiny white kitten.

"My kitty's okay," she crooned. "My kitty's okay." My precious kitten, that I had so longed to touch, clung to Anna and wouldn't let go. At that moment, I realized my little sister had another gift, besides the ability to play the piano by ear alone. She could tame a cat instantly, as soon as she touched it.

I didn't look at Ma as she removed the dead kitten and then led us away from the barn. I cried the rest of the day and into the evening, unable to be consoled. When Ma tucked us into bed that night, she kissed me on the forehead and whispered, "We know what your gift is now, Sarah."

Puzzled, I strained to look at her through swollen eyes.

"You have the Gift of Love. You were born with the most precious gift of all." She drew closer to me to whisper, "I know very well that Anna's kitten was the one killed this morning."

"You're not mad at me for telling a lie?"

Ma smoothed back the hair on my forehead. "I'm proud of you, Sarah. You lied to spare your little sister the grief you're feeling now."

The silence which was filling the room was scented with lilacs and was broken only by the sound of a lonely, unanswered whippoorwill, calling from tree to tree in the moonlit woods beyond our house. I shivered and looked over at Anna, asleep in her bed, with my kitten curled into a fluffy white circle beside her. A spot of moonlight was shining on Ma's face as she too gazed at the tiny cat, so cozy on the quilt, so far removed from the barn where he belonged. I knew then, by looking at Ma's sweet, tolerant smile, that my gift had not come to me out of the blue. It had been there all along, passed down through the generations, from my mother to me.

When Ma covered Anna's kitten with a quilt and then kissed me good-night one final time, I knew nothing could ever change the gift that I had inherited. It didn't matter how many years might go by. It didn't matter how much the world might change in the future. It didn't matter if Ma grew too old to lift her guitar and sing like Patsy Cline or if death began to claim us one by one. Love would last forever.

Ma had given me the most precious gift of all.

Don't Catch a Falling Star

"See a fallin' star, expect another grave." –old Ozark superstition

Lady, don't you know nothin? A fallin' star ain't nothin to be wishin' on. If'n I was you, I'd be lickety-splittin' me a place to hide. Lady, don't you know nothin'?

I caught me one of them fallin' stars once— one mornin' after a big storm that the corn had been bowin' their heads prayin' for—it came explodin' from the sky all fire and ice.

I spotted that little star right down there by the chicken house, on the muddy slippity-slop of the creek, squat-hidin' in the tall wet weeds, washed down from higher country, I reckon.

Well, that little star was curled up in the grass like a scairty-cat caterpillar, its hair all yellow and bright, its hair all slickity and wet, glowin' a little like a lightnin' bug, a little like the sun, a little like a body's soul—yeah, that's it.

I scooped up that little olly-olly oxen in the palm of my hand and cuddled it close and carried it fast to the old woman who lived up the hill. *She'll know what to do with you,* I said. Its eyes, all big and black, watched me all the while.

The old woman was on the porch that mornin', sweepin' and hummin' up the leaves from the storm. *What d'ya got there?* she said.

A surprise fur ya, granny, that's all. Gotta wring it, gotta fluff it, got it first, I said, as I hid it under my shirt. Me and the screen door sneakity-squeaked while the old woman swept hummin' on the porch.

I carried that cold little critter to the kitchen and slippity-plopped it down by the stove. *Gotta get ya fired up,* I said. Its eyes, all big and black, blinked and watched me all the while.

Little drops of water sizzle-danced across the stove as I detangled its yellow wet hair with the old woman's comb.

And then, before ya know it, that little star started perkin' right up, its hair gettin' lighter, its hair gettin' brighter, it hoverin' above the stove and purrin' like a bird-bellied cat, its big black eyes watchin' me all the while.

There were little white lights dippity-deep in them there eyes, and its breath was like a wind whiskin' in from another world.

What have ya come for? I said.
Have ya come to fetch me my very old gold?
Have ya come to fetch me my very own beau?
It purred and watched me all the while.

Now what d'ya got there? the old woman called from the porch.

Me and the screen door peekity-squeaked.
A surprise fur ya granny, I said, *that's all.*
And I held the star out in front of me, its big

black eyes starin' hard at the old woman on the hill.

You devil! the old woman screeched and she whackity-slapped the star with her broom and she beat it she beat it she beat it against the porch until it lay still, curled up like a dead tarantula.

Don't you know nothin'? the old woman screamed and she hit me she hit me she hit me with her broom until I ran down the hill and hid in the cornfield.

The star didn't come to fetch me no gold.

The star didn't come to fetch me no beau.

It just came to fetch the old woman on the hill.

When the next mornin' came looking, that little star was gone too.

Dragged off by a dog, I reckon.

Pecked over by a chicken.

Or gone off to fetch somebody else on some another hill.

Lady, don't you know nothin'?

Mama's Gift

As I was stepping down the dark, narrow steps of the mikvah, I kept hearing the rabbi's wife, right behind me, telling me not to slip, and I kept hearing Mama, a hundred miles and ten years away, saying, "Listen good, Brother James: If my little girl is scairt of the water, she don't *need* to be baptized in this here river." With the voice of the rabbi's wife echoing against the walls and Mama's voice echoing inside my head, I kept wondering why I wasn't afraid to go down into a pool of water now, and I kept wishing Mama was there to see that I wasn't afraid.

But Mama wasn't there. She was back home in the hills. Maybe she was taking down the dry Christmas tree by now. Maybe she was dragging it out across the field and throwing it into the ditch below the pond. Or maybe she was sitting alone in front of the fireplace, rocking back and forth, while all the clocks ticked back and forth on all the walls of the front room.

"Mama, you should get rid of these clocks. It drives me nuts to sit here doing nothing, hearing my life being measured away."

"Your papa loved them clocks. How could I go and toss out something your papa loved so much?"

Mama said that just before my ride came, and I went back to college, through all the fat gray hills and skinny roads that took everyone back to school, back to the world. I was sitting on the rug by the fireplace with my head on my knees. I kept watching Mama rock back and forth. I kept watching her stare into the fire. I kept expecting her to criticize me again, and I kept hoping she wouldn't. Every time she paused in her rocking, I held my breath. She didn't say the words, but I thought I could hear them anyway, going through her head over and over again:

May Jesus Christ forgive you.

***

When I came home from college on Christmas Eve, Maggie was already there. I hadn't seen her since the Christmas before, but that didn't matter because Maggie was always the same. Sometimes it seemed like she only came alive during Christmas, and the rest of the year she was frozen, somewhere out West, with a husband who was a mechanic and a son who was nearly four years old. But I came home for Christmas, and Maggie was alive again. She grabbed me as soon as I stepped onto the porch.

"Now we can get the tree! The tree!" she squealed, jumping up and down, hugging me, pressing her cheek against mine. I tried to stop her before she said anything, but I wasn't quick enough.

"For a minute, I thought Papa was here," she whispered, holding me close. "Don't you wish Papa was here, Sarah May?"

In only five seconds, it seemed like Papa had just died and we were five years younger, going through our first Christmas without him all over again. In only five seconds, Maggie made the front porch of home a sad place to be standing.

Mama opened the screen door and reached out to me. I had seen her two months ago, but she looked different this time. That didn't surprise me—Mama looked different every time I came home from school. The big pumpkin freckles on her face had faded since early autumn, and her mouth and cheeks were sunken in, almost as if she had left her teeth sitting in the fruit jar by her bed. She smiled when she hugged me and brushed the hair away from my eyes.

"Now, Sarah May, what is it? What's ailin' you? What'd you want to tell your mama?"

I wished then that I hadn't started to tell her on the phone. I wished I didn't need to tell her at all.

"Mama, it was nothing. Really."

Maggie, who was still wiping away her tears, grabbed me by the shoulders and lined her eyes up with mine. "You ain't sick, are you, Sarah May?" When I didn't answer, she turned to Mama. "Mama, what are you talkin' 'bout?"

Mama opened the screen door and swept us into the house with one arm. "Sarah May's got somethin' she needs to tell her mama. Ain't that right, girl?"

With those words, Mama rushed us into the hot kitchen. Supper was still on the stove. Maggie smoothed out the red-checkered tablecloth and started placing the best unbent forks by the best un-chipped plates. Mama looked at me for a moment and said that Maggie was right—that I didn't look sick at all—and then she turned away to open the oven door. After she poked the sweet potatoes with a knife, she speared all three of them at once and got them to the table just as one sweet potato split down the middle and fell from the knife and landed in the corn bread. Chicken was frying in the big iron skillet. When its popping sound suddenly changed, Mama looked up and smiled at me. I knew what she was remembering. She was remembering all the times I ran to her as a child, my bare feet slapping against the linoleum floor, to tell her that the chicken was done, saying, *Mama, Mama, the chicken's done. I know by its sound.*

"I used to think that was the eeriest thing," Mama said now, lifting the last crusty, steaming chicken leg from the skillet. "Didn't know whether I had me a genius or a devil." Mama and Maggie laughed at the same time. Maggie said her little boy had caught onto the same trick, and then she pulled out a picture of him to show us. He was as blond and as blue-eyed as she was.

When we sat down at the table, Maggie sighed and stared at Papa's empty chair, but Mama quickly bowed her head and asked me to say the blessing.

I bowed my head. "Baruch—Blessed art Thou, Lord our God, King of the Universe, who bringest forth bread from the Earth."

"In Jesus' name we pray," Mama added, and then she and Maggie looked at me, but they didn't say anything—nothing at all.

Mama poured me a glass of milk with chunks of cream floating on top, just the way Papa always liked it. I said I didn't want any milk, but she kept filling my glass.

"Sarah May, you love milk," she insisted, her face flushed from the heat in the kitchen

"I know. I just don't want any right now." I wanted to say it wouldn't be kosher with chicken, but as soon as I thought of saying it, I knew it wouldn't be the right time. Mama would just look at me blankly and try to say kosher, but it would end up as "kocher" or "kacher," and I would wish I hadn't said anything at all.

"Are you sure you don't want no milk?" Mama asked again. She was looking at my glass now as if the milk were already turning sour.

"I'm sure." And then I added, without knowing why, "It wouldn't be kosher."

Mama stared at me. "Kocher? What kind of talk is that?"

I wished I hadn't said anything at all.

"I know what it is, Mama," Maggie said, who was sitting right beside me. "It's *Jew* talk." I suddenly noticed how different Maggie looked from last year, how deep lines were starting to cut around her mouth and how her belly and thighs were starting to bulge beneath her jeans. She edged her chair closer to mine and started giggling.

"Sarah May—come on—have some milk," she said, as she pushed the glass closer to my plate.

I could hear Papa's clocks ticking in the other room. I knew this wasn't the time to say anything. Even the clocks knew it wasn't time.

"I'm a Jew, Mama," I said, and I didn't know why I had to say it so soon—why I had to go and say it on Christmas Eve.

Mama only stared at me, but Maggie started laughing. She laughed and slapped her thighs with her hands, just the way Papa used to do. When she missed her thigh and hit the table instead, she cried out and waved her fingers into the air, still giggling, still giving me a mischievous sideways glance, her belly popping over the waistband of her jeans. She reminded me of the men down at the general store who sat around the woodstove roasting peanuts for hours at a spell, waving their burnt fingers into the air every time they grabbed a hot peanut from the stove. I almost expected her to slap me on the back and call me a good ole boy.

"I don't understand," Mama said.

"Mama, don't you *know* Sarah May by now? Don't you *know* when she's puttin' you *on*?" Maggie laughed, and then she stopped because she saw the look on Mama's face.

"I don't understand, Sarah May," Mama said. Her face was pale, almost as pale as Papa's when he got sick.

"Don't get upset, Mama. It's nothing. Really."

"What are you sayin,' Sarah May?"

"I'm converting, that's all, Mama." And then, because Mama's face was getting blank again, I added, "I'm *becoming* a Jew."

"That ain't possible. It ain't possible, is it Maggie?"

"It ain't right, Mama. Tell Mama you're teasin', Sarah May. Tell it now, and we'll all have a right good laugh. Go 'head, Sarah May—say it ain't nothin' but a tease."

"It's true, Mama. I've been going to a synagogue at school." I looked down and could see that the sweet potatoes were getting cold and gummy.

"Butter them before they get any colder," I said, as I held out the butter dish to Maggie.

Maggie jumped up, away from the table, scraping the legs of her chair across the linoleum floor. "I ain't never ate with no Jew before," she said. "And I ain't startin' now. Thank God my little boy took with a fever, so he didn't come here and find a Jew for an aunt."

After Maggie ran out of the room, Mama didn't say anything. She merely sat there, her lips tight, and then she began covering her untouched food with her white napkin, just the way she had covered Papa with a white sheet when he died.

"Sarah May, I don't understand," she finally said. "I don't understand how a Christian can become a Jew. It don't make no sense."

"Mama, I'm not a Christian. I've never been a Christian."

"Listen good, Sarah May: I was there when you was baptized. It's true you wasn't baptized in the river, being you was so scairt of the water, but you was baptized anyways. It was just the sprinklin'—but it was still the Holy Baptism. You're a Christian, not a Jew. It ain't possible for you to be a Jew. And may Jesus Christ forgive you for sayin' otherwise."

"Mama, I was only eight years old. I didn't

know what the preacher meant. I didn't know what any of you meant. Mama, I never felt like you felt, or Papa, or Maggie. I tried, Mama, I tried so hard to believe so many times. I used to sit in church and pray that I could believe in Jesus, but I couldn't. I never felt like I belonged there. It was never that way for me. I used to cry in my bed for hours at a time because I couldn't believe, because I felt lost—alone—the only person who didn't believe. You never heard me cry, did you, Mama? I couldn't tell you, Mama. I didn't want to hurt you. I still don't want to hurt you. . . . I was always a Jew, Mama, I just never knew it until a few months ago."

"Sarah May, have you fallen in with some Jew boy?"

"No, Mama. It's nothing like that."

"Did you have a vision, Sarah May? Did you hear God speakin' to you, sayin' the Jews was right and the Christians was wrong?"

"No, Mama, no vision. It's only the way I feel. It's not a question of who's right or who's wrong—it's just how I *feel*. And it's not just Jesus, Mama. My whole outlook is different. I see things differently, that's all, and it doesn't mean you're wrong. Please try to see that."

"I don't understand, Sarah May. It don't make no sense." Mama's lips were starting to quiver. "I never dreamt it was this. When you started to say somethin' on the phone, I tried to figure it out. But

I never dreamt it was this. First, I thought my little girl's sick, and I got sick inside too. But I knew I could commence to makin' you well as soon as you got home. And then I thought, what if my little girl's homesick? What if she is just scairt of that school and wants to quit college? And then I thought that would be the worst thing. But then I got to thinkin' it wouldn't be so bad to have my Sarah May at home, and you could work in the shirt factory and marry some boy from 'round here. And then I thought, what if my baby is goin' to have a baby, and some city boy off at that college won't marry her? And I wisht your Papa was here to make him marry you. But I never dreamt it was this. I wish it was anythin' but this. You're goin' to burn in hell, Sarah May." She was crying now, crying almost as hard as when Papa died. "It ain't *safe*. It ain't *safe* to be a Jew, Sarah May. Don't you know that by now?" Mama looked away from me and then slowly pushed her chair away from the table. When she got up and left the room, she walked with one hand on her lower back, as if she were hurting from carrying a heavy, unborn child.

***

I could hear Mama crying late into the night as I lay in my old bed, where I used to cry, where I used to wonder why I couldn't believe, and why it wasn't the same for me as it was for Mama and Papa and Maggie.

When I first heard her crying, I went into the hall and listened at her door. I tried to open it, but it was locked. I wondered where she had ever found the key. No door in our house had ever been locked before.

I turned away and stood alone in the moonlit hall. Mama's crying was softer now, soft enough for me to hear Papa's clocks ticking back and forth in the front room. Papa had always collected clocks, while Mama had always collected pictures. They lined the hall on each side of me now—a hodgepodge of modern wallet-sized school pictures and framed portraits. No one knew exactly why Mama loved pictures so much, but we thought it might be because they were so rare in her family after a house fire over a hundred years ago. Nothing had survived that fire, except for a single portrait of my great-great grandmother, who had died in the flames. Her picture, which usually hung neatly by Mama's door, was hanging lopsided on the wall tonight, as if someone had brushed it in passing or had taken it down for a moment and then had put it back without bothering to hang it straight.

I stepped closer to the portrait and peered at it. More than a century had passed since the fire, but the picture's black charred frame and broken glass had never been replaced. My great-great-grandmother, with a tendril of dark hair curling over one cheek and a secretive half-smile, was looking back at me through the cracked glass. If it weren't for her, I might have thought I wasn't even related to Mama and Papa and Maggie. Everyone in the family had always been blond. But my great-great grandmother was different. She looked like me—a dark-haired silhouette on a moonlit wall surrounded by sun-freckled blonds. She looked out of place here—as out of place as I had always been.

Mama was still crying. I checked her door one more time before I returned to my empty room. When I sat down on the edge of the bed, I drew back the crocheted lace curtains Mama had made when she was a young bride. They had yellowed with age, but they were as perfect as they had always been. I wiped the cold, squeaky glass with the palm of my hand and looked out the window.

The first snow of the year had started falling shortly after sunset. I wondered if Mama knew. I wondered if she could hear it slipping softly across the tin roof above us. I wondered if she knew how it was covering the fields and hills behind our house, how it was draping the pine trees and sage grass in white. A board on the floor behind me suddenly creaked. It was Maggie, standing there, watching me, wrapped up in the coat that Papa had given her six Christmases before.

"Sarah May. . . ." Her whisper was like the snow slipping across the tin roof. "We need to get Mama a tree."

As I was pulling a pair of jeans over my pajamas, Maggie touched me gently on the arm. "I think Mama's finally asleep now," she said, "so be real quiet-like."

And then we were going across the field behind our house, just as we always did on the day before Christmas, except this time the moon lit our way instead of the sun. It was snowing more heavily now, but the air around us was warm and still, almost as if the night itself were holding its breath, watching the snowflakes slowly fall, watching us slowly cross the field. Maggie led the way, just like always, until she stopped and pointed with her bow-saw to the far corner of the field.

"'Member that patch of little bitty pines over yonder?"

Yes, I remembered. But I wondered if Maggie remembered what she had said at the supper table. It seemed like she didn't remember it at all—that she was just the same again.

We jumped over a deep gully. I slipped in the snow when I landed on the other side. Maggie giggled and bent over to help me back up.

"You do that every single time, Sarah May," she said, as she pulled me to my feet, just like always.

We started off again, and Maggie dropped back to walk by my side. She began talking about her little boy, who was four years old, and her husband, who was a mechanic. When she was telling me again how much she missed them, she suddenly stopped and said, "I heard everything you told Mama," and then she ran up the steep bank of the pond and didn't slip once on the snow-covered dirt and gravel.

"Come on up," she called out. She looked like a little girl again, standing up there all alone, dwarfed by the cold black sky and the silhouette of the snow-draped pine tree towering high above her head. After she helped me up the steep embankment, she sat down and started throwing rocks into the pond. I sat down beside her and listened to them plop into the water. When one of the rocks skipped across the surface of the water several times, she clapped her hands and laughed. The night all around us was still holding its breath, watching us.

"You was never like us," Maggie said suddenly. "You was always different," she added, as she threw another rock into the water. "You know, my Bobby likes me just the way I am. He told me he never wants me to change. He said that the day we met and the day we married." She reached across me and plucked up a round stone from the snow and popped it into the water. The night listened to the sound.

"You was always different, Sarah May. Everybody says that. Everybody knows that. You don't even talk like us. I've been livin' outside of the hills for six year now, and I still talk like us, but you don't. Sarah May? Why can't you be like us? Mama's been cryin' down there all night, and Papa must be cryin' too." She took a deep breath. "Don't be different, Sarah May—tell me it's all a tease, and it'll be Christmas again, just like it always was. Don't be different, Sarah May, tell me you're not a Jew."

"Maggie, I can't."

When Maggie started sobbing, I wondered if her little boy sobbed in the same way. "You're bein' mean, Sarah May. You're d-doin' it to hurt us—you wanna spoil Christmas for everybody, so nobody'll have no fun. Tell me it's a tease, Sarah May—just tell me—it don't have to be true—just tell me."

I stroked Maggie's soft blond hair and remembered the rabbi asking me if I could be subconsciously trying to hurt my family. I stroked her hair, her soft blond hair, and I could feel the night, the soft black night, holding its breath all around us.

"It ain't nothin' but a tease, Maggie, that's all it is."

As soon as I said it, Maggie jumped up with a

laugh and whirled around on the pond bank, hugging herself. She stopped abruptly and surveyed the white hills in every direction.

"Sarah May, 'member that poem you made up when you was little? 'Member that poem you used to say? You have to 'member it, Sarah May, 'cause I do. I always think it to myself." She swallowed and then she recited it, pronouncing each syllable slowly, almost as if she were spelling out all the words.

> "The Ozarks roll on and on to the east and west,
> In the place where the world began,
> In the place that God loves best."

She looked at me with tears in her eyes. "That's still true, ain't it, Sarah May?"

"Yes, Maggie," I answered. She laughed, grabbed me by the arm, and we went flying down the pond bank together, never slipping once in the snow. A moment later, we were crossing the field to where that patch of little pines was growing, with Maggie walking in front of me, just like always.

***

Maggie left Mama's when the needles of the Christmas tree were starting to drop off and scatter across the floor. We flagged down the bus on the highway, and Maggie hugged Mama and me and told us she'd see us next Christmas. Then she stepped up into the bus, lugged her suitcase down the aisle, and pressed her nose against the back window, waving goodbye with both hands. Within a few seconds, the bus was grinding up the hill, and Maggie was gone, frozen out West, once again.

***

Mama sat in her rocker by the fireplace and creaked back and forth while all the clocks ticked back and forth on the walls of the front room. I hadn't seen Mama cry since Christmas Eve. Every night since then we had sat together by the fire. Mama had rocked back and forth, and Maggie had talked about the old days, sometimes confusing her son's childhood with her own. Mama wouldn't say much until Maggie had yawned and gone off to bed.

Mama's voice was gentle. Mama's voice was soft. I felt as if I were talking with the rabbi, and I was trying to answer all the questions all over again. Mama kept asking and I kept explaining. Mama kept saying, *May Jesus Christ forgive you,* and I kept thinking, *You're never going to understand, never.*

But the night after Maggie left, when Mama was sitting in her chair, she rocked back and forth without saying a word. I told her she should get rid of those clocks, and she reminded me how much Papa had loved them. Then she stopped her rocking, and I held my breath and waited for her to say, "May Jesus Christ forgive you." She didn't say anything, but I thought I could hear the words anyway.

Mama reached into her dress pocket and handed me something wrapped in white tissue.

"Merry Christmas, Sarah May."

"Mama, you already gave me too much."

But Mama leaned forward, almost smiling, waiting for me to open it. I folded back the tissue and held the gift toward the light. The ragged edges of the book in my hands were crumbling with age and soot. The tips of my fingers were already stained black.

"What kind of writin' is that, Sarah May?"

"Mama. . . ."

"What d'ya call it, Sarah May?"

"It's Hebrew, Mama. It's a Hebrew prayer book. Where did you get it?"

Mama leaned back and started rocking again. "Hebrew. I was hopin' you'd know. Did Jesus talk Hebrew?"

"Mama, where did you get it?"

"Listen good, Sarah May. You was always different. Everybody knew that. Everybody said that. But, Sarah May, I never heard you cryin' in the night. I *never* heard you. If I'd heard you, I would've told you. . . . *Maybe* I would've told you."

Mama stopped rocking and stared up at the ceiling. She sighed then, as if someone had just told her something she didn't want to hear. "That there prayer book," Mama said, eyeing me closely, "was my great-granny's."

I stared at Mama and started to speak, but she leaned forward in her chair and put her fingers to my lips. "The fire that killed her was no accident, Sarah May," she whispered. "She died a long time ago, 'fore my folks ever came to these here hills. *Nobody 'round here will ever know.*" When Mama leaned back and started rocking again, I suddenly heard the clocks ticking, as if they had just started ticking after stopping to listen to Mama.

The next morning my ride came, and I went back to school, through all the fat gray hills and skinny roads that took everyone back to school, back to the world. Three days later, the rabbi's wife was telling me not to slip as I started down the mikvah steps, and I could hear Mama, a hundred miles and ten years away, telling the preacher I was scared of the water. With Mama's voice echoing in my head—and her great-grandmother's prayer book clutched in my hand—I kept wishing Mama could see that the water didn't scare me anymore—that I was headed for a river which would carry me safely home.

The Ozarks

An Objective Description:

The Ozark Plateau is located in southern Missouri, northern Arkansas, and northeastern Oklahoma. The Ozarks are often referred to as mountains, but they are actually hills—the result of centuries of down-cutting into the escarpment. The average elevation is 1500 feet.

Trees and wild animals are abundant in the Ozark area. Pines, cedars, sycamores, oaks and dogwoods cover the sandy hills, and deer, coyotes, possums, bobwhites, whippoorwills, and raccoons populate the woods. Lakes, rivers, and streams are also prevalent.

The Ozark Plateau has a mild climate. The average annual temperature is 68 degrees; the average annual precipitation is 55 inches. Summer days are hot and humid, but the humidity often contributes to chilly summer nights. Autumn brings drizzling rain and mist. Winter varies from sunny to icy. Spring brings thunderstorms, rain, and dogwood blossoms.

Many people in the Ozarks are descendants of the Appalachian mountaineers who moved west to the Ozark region in the 1800s. Agriculture has been the traditional mainstay of the people.

During the last 30 years, however, farming has become increasingly unprofitable, and many young people have been forced to leave the area to find employment elsewhere.

The Ozarks: A Subjective Description

When you grow up in the Ozark Mountains, you are cursed for life. They leave an impression on you that you never forget. You become a person who feels empty and vulnerable when there are no hills in sight or bobwhites and whippoorwills in sound. You feel homeless without trees, and when you leave the mountains, you look back at them and want to return before you've even left them completely behind.

You are cursed for life. If you stay, you are sentenced to work that never pays, to years of drudgery that weigh you down and break your back and line your face before you're thirty.

You are cursed for life. If you leave, you hate where you go. You hate the stench and noise and congestion of the city. You dream of damp, earthy air, of miles and miles of rolling wooded hills and of clear, silent winter nights.

You are cursed for life. If you stay, you see the autumn mountains exploding in color and wave after wave of light sweeping through the trees. But then the fog and rain set in, and everything seems to go wrong. You search for missing goats in the woods at night. You call their names and trip over rocks and brush, and sometimes you find them—torn by coyotes or trapped in a ditch or hung up on a fence or bloated in a field. If they're still alive, their ears twitch and they cry out when you whisper their names. You have to shoot them to stop the suffering—yours and theirs.

And when you leave—and you have to leave in order to live—you think of those days when you were a child, when the Ozarks rolled on and on forever, when "the City" was a single place in the outside world, and you wonder why you have to be cursed, why you can't leave in peace, why you always have to return. You never figure it out. You just cry when the land rolls flat and the city lights come into view.

Marooned

The Ozark Mountains were different back then, in the early 1960s, when I was a kid, when Mama and Daddy started storing food and water in our cellar and began waiting for the Atomic War to blow us out of orbit. We had electricity, but there weren't many televisions or telephones or major highways, and everybody was still alone, in their own neck of the woods, hanging onto the side of some cedar-rock mountain or hiding by a creek in some dark, lost holler.

We lived down in one of those hollers, and it was a good enough place, with pine trees so tall and thick that our tiny house seldom saw the sun, and a creek so dark and spooky that the goats were afraid to cross it alone. Yes, it was a good enough place, but my brother and I longed for something else. We yearned and burned for the stars, for the blackness of outer space, for all the other worlds *out there*, just beyond our fingertips. To keep a better eye on the universe, we built our own little observatory on the highest hill above our house. Its "walls" were only a low circle of smooth, flat rocks, but we would perch up there every clear frog-sung summer night, our heads craning upward, our lips curled into sweet smiles, basking under the stars like goats basking in a sunny paradise.

    Davey and I were strange little kids back then. Everybody said so. Some said we were strange because of Daddy, because he had always wanted to go to college, and because he drove to the city once a month and hauled back a bushel of books for Mama and Davey and me. Some said we were strange because our holler was so dark and lonely that it wasn't natural at all. They even whispered it made me and Davey walk funny, always on tiptoe, our necks stretched to the sky as if we were trying to catch a little sunlight. Maybe that's why they looked at us all funny-eyed whenever we walked into Walker's General Store on hot summer days, our sweaty hands clasped firmly together. Or maybe they looked at us all funny-eyed because Davey and I never stopped chattering about stars and spaceships and far-flung planets. You see, the books Daddy brought home from the city were gothic books for Mama and philosophy books for himself and science fiction books for Davey and me, and somehow Davey and I got it into our heads that the Ozarks were closer to the stars than any other part of the world and that we were the hub for all the interstellar traffic in our part of the galaxy.

    Davey and I knew the truth about the world back then. We knew the truth about the falling stars that shot across the Ozarks every black summer night: They weren't stars at all—and certainly not meteors—they were spaceships humming home to their bases in the Ozark Mountains. We knew the truth about the slicked-up city man who dallied down at Walker's General Store every Wednesday afternoon: He wasn't a man at all—and certainly not a salesman—he was a government robot recruiting colonists for Alpha Centauri.

Davey and I knew the truth about the world, and so we watched the stars every summer night. We dreamed and we waited, searching the skies until our necks ached. When we spotted an incoming spaceship, streaking across the black night like a meteor, we jumped up and tried to flag it down with fruit-jar lanterns filled with lightning bugs. All the spaceships always hummed on by, and we were always left alone on the hill, but we never despaired.

"Did you see that?" my brother would say. "I do believe that ship flashed a light at us."

Yes, we knew the truth about the world, and so we would stand around the pop machine at Walker's General Store every Wednesday afternoon, holding hands, patiently waiting on tiptoe for the slicked-up government robot to finish his bottle of icy orange pop and whisk us off to a shiny new spaceship. The robot's station wagon always rumbled off in a blast of dust, and we were always left standing alone by the pop machine, but when we walked home together, tiptoeing down the dusty road, tiptoeing through the dark woods, hollering for the goats to come home, we never despaired.

"Did you hear that, Cissy?" my brother would say when we reached the barn. "The government robot-man said, 'See you next week, kids.'" We nodded at each other and milked the goats a little faster as we discussed the mile-high library they were building in the shining red seas of Alpha Centauri.

Yes, we knew the truth about the world, and so when Mama and Daddy started putting canned beans and corn and bottles of water into our cellar and started talking about surviving an Atomic War, Davey and I got a little confused. I pulled on Daddy's arm and looked up at him and said, "Listen, Daddy, why don't we just build us a ship and head on out to Alpha Centauri? It'd seem a bit might easier."

It was then that Daddy looked at me and Davey all funny-eyed. "Aren't you ten by now, Cissy?" he asked, and then he hurried to the house, calling for Mama. Davey and I just shrugged our shoulders and started designing our own personal spaceship.

When Daddy went into the city the next month, he didn't come back with a big haul of books. Instead, he came back with big rolls of wire and big prongs of metal, and Davey and I breathed a little easier that Daddy was finally going to build us a spaceship. But then Daddy lifted out one of those round TV sets, and that was almost as good. It was the wonderful, glorious instrument that would bring us our first contact with another world—the wonderful, glorious instrument that would show us our first moving pictures of Alpha Centauri.

It took a spell to get that TV set ready. Daddy strung wire from our observatory high on the hill down to the tin roof of our house, and he fiddled and conversed with all the knobs and tubes for over three days. On Daddy's okey-dokey, Davey and I perched in front of the TV, our necks stretched forward, our lips curled into smiles, patiently waiting for our first glimpse of the shining red seas of Alpha Centauri.

The sun was just fixing to set on the hillside above our house when the evening news finally popped through all the static. Davey and I sat in silence as we listened to the news of the day. And then it happened—the thing that changed our lives and told us the awful truth about the world.

Some slicked-up city man appeared on the screen and said: *"It is the hope of the President that the United States will successfully place a man on the moon by the end of this decade."*

The MOON!

Davey and I stared at each other for just a second, and then we tore out of the house together, past Daddy in his chair, past Mama at the stove, and we charged up the hill like a couple of dog-nipped goats. We stumbled when we got to the top and stared at all the prongs and wires that now claimed our observatory—at the observatory that had brought us our first contact with another world. We stretched our necks to the sky and swallowed hard. It was going to be another clear, frog-sung summer night. The stars were already shining and glimmering like a million lightning bugs. It was then that Davey and I slumped to the ground and looked at each other all wild-eyed.

"Can you believe it, Cissy?" Davey said, trying hard to swallow the lump in his throat. "Can you believe them folks is so *primitive*? They ain't even been to the *moon* yet."

We kept staring up at the stars, even though Daddy was calling for us. The stars seemed to be staring back at us, their eyes blinking as much as ours, in rhythm to the frogs and crickets and whippoorwills. But we were blinking our eyes to hold back our tears, while the stars were only blinking theirs to keep a straight face, to keep their snickers from snorting into laughter. We had never known them to be such strangers before.

We got up and started down the hill separately, no longer on tiptoe, our heads bowed down like a couple of sad-eyed goats defeated by a damp and cloudy day. Just before we answered Daddy's call, Davey turned to me.

"You know, Ciss, I feel real lonesome."

I knew just how he felt. The world had changed and would never be the same again. It had shrunk into a tiny little ball, floating all alone in a cold-black night. We weren't the hub of the universe anymore. We couldn't flag down a spaceship. The robot-man in the station wagon wouldn't be back for us. We were marooned.

Our only consolation was the smell of Mama's fried chicken, and we let out a belly-yell to let Daddy know we were coming back down. Coming back down to that itty bitty house down in the holler, hidden somewhere in the Ozark Mountains, somewhere on a lonely planet, somewhere at the edge of one little galaxy, all alone in the night. We could see the glow of the TV set through the window—the wonderful, glorious instrument that had already begun to change our lives. It had shown us the primitive world which lay beyond the Ozark Mountains— the primitive world that had all the telephones and televisions and Atomic bombs and no memories of the shining red seas of Alpha Centauri.

Who's Afraid of the Big Bad Goats?

Since the number of goats in the United States is rapidly increasing, I, as a responsible citizen, feel obligated to divulge certain pieces of information pertaining to these creatures. The information that I have accumulated over the years is painstakingly accurate. I only hope that others can benefit from my personal experience.

As the keeper of a herd, I have seen all kinds of goats. My barn has housed as many as two hundred of them at one time. Some come with small, tattered suitcases; others come with no suitcase at all. Many of them are pregnant and have run away from home. They stand out on the road and scream for admittance into the herd. I let them through; I feed them; I give them shelter; I even deliver their kids. Sometimes I receive milk or money in return; all too often, I receive a kiss on the cheek or a carefully planned teardrop. Sometimes I gain a friend for life; sometimes my boarders leave without a word when they hear about the free alfalfa hay up the road. I have seen all kinds of goats, and here, as a public service, I will elaborate on four important types: the Rough-Tough, the Kissy-Kissy, the Tattle-Tale, and the Nirvani-Nanny.

TYPE A: THE ROUGH-TOUGH.

The Rough-Tough Nanny weighs in at 275 pounds. She has robust, muscular shoulders, long horns, and thick jaws. She stands out on the road and demands a private room. I cautiously open the gate. She swaggers through, dumps her black suitcase at my feet and glares at the goats that are lounging around the yard. Immediate panic grips the herd. A few nannies bury their heads in their hooves and cry hysterically, while others giggle or simply faint. If we are lucky, at least one nanny has been highly trained for situations of this sort, and she acts quickly, lining the others up into military formation and putting them all at attention. Silence descends upon the herd. The nannies twitch nervously in line as the Rough-Tough Nanny slowly struts around and examines her new company. If anyone dares to look her in the eye, she flattens the offender and pins her to the ground until an apology has been given and accepted. After beating up a few of the old, crippled goats—just for fun—the hefty 275-pounder returns to me and says in a sugary, high-pitched voice, "I'm especially fond of cracked corn sweetened with molasses. My water must be warm in the winter, of course, and refreshingly cool in the summer. I'd like a dry room upstairs, if you don't mind, with a view of the orchard. I can only pay a pint of milk a day, but I'll keep those dumbos in line for you as well. I'm sure that will suffice. Shall we go to my room? And don't forget my valise, s'il vous plaît."

As I carry her suitcase, she struts at my side and bumps into me every few feet, letting everyone know that the Person now has a new best friend.

TYPE B: THE KISSY-KISSY.

The Kissy-Kissy Nanny hangs on the front gate with her hooves wrapped around the barbed wire. Tears stream down her face as she beats her head against a post.

"Oh, my God!" she cries out, "I'm SO lonely! Please let me in!"

I open the gate, and she charges through, throwing her front hooves around my neck and kissing me on both cheeks. "Oh, I *love* you, Person! Let's be friends forever! Oh, Please! Please!"

Her fear of goats (capraphobia) forces me to take her by the hoof and show her around the yard. When she sees the woods, she tightens her grip on my hand and begins to jump up and down.

"I'm *scared* to go into the woods alone," she wails. "Oh, *please* go with me—please!!"

If I make the mistake of nodding, she throws her hoof around my neck and cries, "Oh, I *love* you, Person! Let's be friends forever!" She kisses me again, letting everyone know that the Person now has a new best friend.

TYPE C: THE TATTLE-TALE.

The Tattle-Tale Nanny politely knocks at my gate. She gives me a nod and requests a meal and a place to nap. As I take her to the eating area, I become somewhat suspicious of her disposition when she taps me on the shoulder and whispers in my ear, "Someone around here stinks."

My suspicions are confirmed at milking time. "Psssssst! Person!" she whispers softly, "I have a list," and then she names, in uncanny alphabetical order, all the nannies "who don't give a drop."

And, of course, when the herd finds a hole in the fence and races to a neighbor's orchard, I can depend upon Tattle-Tale:

"Oh, my God, Person!!" she screams hysterically from a mile away. "Bad Nannies! Bad Nannies! They done did it this time! Done broke down the fence! I tried to stop'em! My God, Person, what will we do now?" (She quickly swallows a stem from the neighbor's apple tree as she comes into view.)

When I go to recover the delinquent nannies, Tattle-Tale tags along at my side, sticking her nose up into the air at the bad nannies and letting everyone know that the Person now has a new best friend.

TYPE D: THE NIRVANI-NANNY.

    I never see the Nirvani-Nanny at my gate—she just mysteriously appears in the herd one day, with her long white beard blowing in the breeze and a perpetual smile on her lips. When I ask her where she has come from, she snorts cynically. With half-closed eyes, she answers, "Don't you know?"

    Being quite convinced that she was a person in a former life, the Nirvani-Nanny is pleased that she has moved up to a higher state in her present incarnation. She spends her time basking in the sun, chewing her cud, and smiling. A small group gathers around her constantly, listening attentively to her words of wisdom.

    "Person," she says to me, "why run to and fro all day with buckets and pails? Relax, my child. Sit in the sun. Enjoy the spiritual life. We have no need of earthly buckets, of earthly grain, of earthly water." She laughs. "None of this will matter tomorrow." Putting one hoof lazily around my shoulders, she takes me through the yard, telling me that I can be a goat too someday—if I'm good—if I'm kind—if I'm kind to her. I quickly give her a handful of grain. She munches on the corn and continues to stroll with me around the yard, showing everyone the grain and letting everyone know that the Person now has a new best friend.

I must stress, as a final note, that the goat population of the world is highly complex and varied. I have attempted to describe, at great personal risk, only the most important types of goats that I have encountered in my days as Person and Keeper of a goat herd.

Lynda Eymann

The Wild October Sea

The October sky is gray. It looks like a wrinkled rag that has been hung out to dry, abandoned, flapping in the wind, the worn weave of the fabric filtering the light of the morning sun. The October sea is gray too. It heaves restlessly across the horizon, folding and flinging and flipping itself, again and again, determined to touch the wet, gray fabric of the sky.

Samantha is walking alone on the abandoned beach. Her bare toes are sinking into the wet sand; the frayed cuffs of her jeans are dragging through the foamy water; her tangled red hair is wrapping around her neck and whipping toward the sea. In one hand, she clutches the unopened letter that will decide her fate. She grips the letter tightly, trying to control its blue flapping wings. When she turns to face the sea, a lone seagull squeals and dips into a swelling wave. A twinge of regret rolls through her stomach: She will never hear or watch another seagull again.

She clutches the letter harder. He never understood. He never understood how she could love seagulls so much.

It's the sound, Stanley. It's the sound. They're saying something—something I need to understand. I don't know what it is, but it makes me want to twirl and dance and leap across the sea.

He had frowned at her, his thick eyebrows furrowing into question marks. *They're pesky birds, disgusting birds.*

And because she loved him so much—because the sound of his voice resonating in her heart made her want to twirl and dance and leap across the sea—she had agreed.

The ocean crashes against her now, soaking her legs and jeans, weighing her down. She stumbles backward and looks from side to side. The beach to the south is empty. It stretches as far as she can see, all the way to the northern border of Spain. The tourists and summer residents left over a week ago, swarming back to work, back to their homes in Germany and England and northern France. When the white seagull suddenly sweeps across the gray sky directly in front of her, she wonders what it's still doing here, all alone. The other seagulls have already abandoned the beach. Why is it still here?

She looks in the other direction, back to the summer resort of Saint Cyprien, squinting as she scans the familiar jagged line of red-tiled roofs and white-stuccoed walls. Most of the windows of the houses and stores are boarded up. Most of their eyes are closed. No one is watching her. Not even the grocer's daughter, Annette, is watching her.

She's playing alone at the edge of the shore, oblivious to the sea and sky, oblivious to anyone on the beach, bouncing a pink and yellow beach ball high into the air, aiming for the sky, her thin, bony shoulders flapping like wings. With a pang, Samantha realizes she'll never give Annette another English lesson. She lifts one hand and waves to her. The little girl doesn't notice; she just slaps the beach ball as hard as she can and scampers to one side to avoid an incoming wave. Samantha drops her hand and whispers goodbye, but her whisper is quickly snatched away by the sea.

    She turns to face the ocean again, her chin tilted upward. Digging her heels into the sand, she leans back against the force of the flapping gray sky and balances precariously in the wind. As the lone seagull calls out across the rolling waves, she feels another rolling twinge in her stomach: She will never stand here again. She will never paint this day.

    She clutches the letter harder, wishing he had liked her paintings, just once.

    I'm afraid they're a bit unimaginative. Where's the thought behind them? The inspiration? Where's your sense of history, evolution, revolution? He had looked at her warily then, biting the inside of his cheek, disappointed, displeased.

And because she loved him so much—because she could never paint what she felt for him—what it felt like when she burrowed her head into his chest and listened to the gentle surging of his submerged heart—she had agreed, agreed that her paintings were incomplete, ill-conceived, mundane.

A wave slams against her. She can hear Annette's voice far in the distance, calling to her.

Hello!

The little girl's voice is bobbing up and down on the wind, almost pulled out to sea.

Hello! Annette calls again. She's holding her beach ball high in the air now, high above her head, on display for the whole world, almost losing her balance under its weight.

Samantha lifts one hand in approval. *Splendid*, she calls back, and then she watches as Annette prances off across the beach, batting the ball into the air, chasing its pink and yellow stripes across the gray sky.

Splendide, Samantha whispers to herself in French, letting the word swirl softly in her mouth. *Splendide.* She holds the letter close to her heart. He never understood. He never understood why she loved languages so much. She first came to France only four years ago, when she was seventeen, to live with her father when her mother died. Until she met Stanley, she had been proud that she had learned French so easily and so well, that she could often pass as a native speaker. She had learned Italian and German just as easily, and she was beginning to study Spanish when she met Stanley.

Why are you speaking all these languages? If you're not doing something with them, if you're not studying Voltaire, Dante, Goethe?

He didn't know, didn't understand, that she would have learned the languages for the sounds alone—for the slipping and sliding—for the rising and falling—for the rolling and flowing—just for the intrinsic beauty of the words themselves.

Ridiculous.

And because she loved him so much—because she could never translate what she felt for him—could never translate the sound of his resonating voice or the sound of his sweetly surging heart—she had agreed, agreed that she should be doing more with her life than watching seagulls and dabbling in watercolors and mimicking words.

You're losing yourself, her father told her months ago.

But her father doesn't understand. No one understands. Stanley is her other half, torn away from her at the beginning of time. A billion years to find him—only a lifetime to love him. He is her lover, her brother, her long-lost soul.

And so she faces the gray sea, holding the blue letter in her hand. It keeps flapping away from her, desperate to escape from her grasp. She takes a deep breath of the salty air. For a moment, she feels a swelling of hope. What if she is wrong? What if the letter says something else? What if it says *yes, yes, yes!?*

She runs her fingertips across the paper, tracing the raised bumps of his handwriting. A sudden gust of wind sucks her breath and her hope away and leaves a pit in her stomach. She can tell by the tiny bumps on the paper that he wrote the words in very small letters, pressing the paper very hard with his pen. His handwriting has become progressively smaller and harder in recent months. She knows what this letter will say.

She closes her eyes, bows her head, and lifts the flapping letter to her nose. Even in the salty air, it smells like ink and cigarettes; even in the salty air, it smells like Stanley Wald. Her lungs and her heart ache at the scent, and she pretends, for a moment, that he still loves her, that he still wants her, that she will soon be flying across the wild October sea. She opens her eyes and then suddenly rips open the letter, fighting to control its blue flapping wings, bracing herself. Her legs almost buckle as the wind and the sea slam against her.

DON'T COME, DON'T COME, the letter says. *DON'T COME.*

She can't breathe as she reads the rest of the letter, as she stands facing the wild October sea and the flapping gray sky. The seagull is flapping and shrieking at the sea. Annette is flapping and shrieking at her ball. The letter is flapping and shrieking at her heart.

She drops to her knees and scoops out a hole in the wet sand. Gently, with the tips of her fingers, she pokes the letter into the hole and covers it before it can fly away.

DON'T COME, DON'T COME, DON'T COME. She buries the letter as deeply as she can into the wet, oozing sand.

When she stands up and faces the sea, another wave rushes in and surrounds her. It soaks her to the waist this time, almost pulling her down. She looks from side to side. Except for Annette, the beach is empty, all the way to Spain in one direction—and all the way to Saint Cyprien in the other. She begins moving rapidly now, faster than the pain, stripping off her blouse and her heavy wet jeans, revealing a bathing suit beneath. She wants it to look like an accident. She doesn't want her father to know. If her father finds out, if he knows the reason, he will blame Stanley. She can almost see her father flying halfway around the world to beat Stanley to death with his grief-swollen fists. In spite of everything, she can't bear the thought of Stanley being hurt. She folds her clothes neatly on the beach, away from the foamy, ragged edge of the sea. They will think it's an accident, she is sure. Even a strong swimmer like herself could be easily lost on this wild October day.

The waves fight against her at first. They keep pushing her back, rejecting her, refusing to be a part of her plan. But she sucks in her stomach and heaves out her chest and runs in slow motion in the water, away from the pain on the shore.

DON'T COME. DON'T COME. DON'T COME.

The waves surge against her, almost knocking her down. She grits her teeth and clenches her fists and dives directly into the wild October waves.

She is surprised that the sea feels so warm against her face. As the thought of a warm death consoles her, an angry wave suddenly slaps her across her face with its wet hand, and then it seems to apologize and starts pulling her out by her waist, dancing her farther and farther out, away from the pain on the shore. Samantha looks back at Saint Cyprien. Beyond the swelling waves, she can still see the red-tiled roofs and the boarded-up windows; she can still see the closed eyes of the town. Annette's pink and yellow beach ball is flying higher and higher into the air, and the seagull is dipping again and again into the gray ocean. She closes her eyes, determined to separate herself from the sounds of the seagull and the little girl as they squeal with delight.

The sea is rolling her out, farther and farther out. She's being pulled to the center of the earth now, back into its womb. The seagull calls out again, from far away. Will it be the last sound she hears? Will she regret this then? Will she wish she isn't going to die? The seagull screams again, a little closer than before, and she feels another twinge in her stomach. She opens her eyes, surprised at the gathering swarm of gray waves around her, surprised that she is so far from the shore.

Maybe she should go back. Maybe she should go back and wait for her father to come home from Paris. Maybe he can help her. But then she remembers the pain waiting for her on the beach, and she knows she can't go back. Nothing can help her. If she goes back, she will only spend another sixty years growing older and older, never waking from the terrible nightmare, still hurting, still yearning, still not believing—never believing—that Stanley Wald doesn't love her anymore.

A wave sweeps her high into the air. He was the one who said they were each other's half, torn from each other at the beginning of time. He was the one who said they were soul-mates. He was the one who said he would love her forever. And now he wrote to say: *I feel suffocated. You're too dependent. You have no interests of your own. I need a more intelligent and artistic woman.*

A *more intelligent and artistic woman.* What was she, before she met him? How had she failed to show him who she was?

Another wave lifts her higher into the air. She can almost touch the wet, gray fabric of the sky now. She did everything she could to please him. She wanted to be what he wanted—someone like himself—someone beautiful and brilliant and sensitive. She gave so much, loved him so much, that she was shocked whenever she looked into a mirror and saw her own face instead of his.

Failed. She had failed. She had found the only man she would ever love—the only man who was her other half—the only man she was destined to love—and she had failed to keep him. She isn't beautiful. She isn't brilliant. She isn't artistic. She isn't anything. And now she has nothing. Only the pain—the terrible pain—the never-ending pain—is waiting for her on the shore.

I feel suffocated. You're too dependent.

As she remembers those words—the words she buried on the beach—she plunges into the next wave and forces herself to inhale the water. The sea shoots through her nose and down her throat and burns her to the heels of her feet. Coughing, she struggles to the surface, claws at her hair to unwrap it from her neck, and looks back at the town. She gags and looks away. She will let herself be pulled out. She will close her eyes and drift away. She will lie back in the arms of the sea and drown in her sleep without knowing, without feeling. It will be a dream, only a dream, away from the nightmare on the shore.

***

Samantha is drifting farther and farther away from the abandoned beach. As she squints at the flapping gray sky, she wonders why the sky seems so bright when it is so gray. A wave lifts her high into the air. She kicks her legs to stay with it, surprised to find that her legs already feel heavy and weak, not like her legs at all. She stares at her hands beneath the surface of the water. Her fingers look unfamiliar to her, spongy and swollen and disconnected. She closes her eyes and turns to lie back on the sea. She wonders if she will wash up on a beach in Spain. She wonders if her body will be bloated and white, if maggots will be clinging to her glazed green eyes, if a strand of slimy seaweed will be wrapped around her neck. Will a child like Annette find her? She looks back at the shore then, to catch a final glimpse of Annette and her beach ball. But the shore is empty. She can only spot the seagull, sailing just above the waves, screeching again and again at the sea. A wave suddenly sweeps over her, sucks her down, and then slaps her back to the surface. As she flings her head from side to side and gasps for air, she sees Annette's pink and yellow beach ball in the distance, near the shore, tumbling across the gray sea like a bloated clown. She feels sorry for the little girl, sorry that she has lost her ball. And then she sees something else, something being tossed in the waves, and she knows that it's Annette, far away, reaching up to the sky stiff-fingered, trying to leap away from the sea. She knows it's not possible to see her so clearly at this distance, but she is sure she can even see Annette's little face, her big blue eyes ringed by bands of white, her mouth distorted, turning inside out, her screams swallowed by the sea.

Samantha closes her eyes.

She can't go back. If she goes back, she will have to live. If she goes back, she will have to feel the pain on the shore. Everything is numb out here. Everything is safe. She can't go back.

But she opens her eyes and sees Annette's face again, far away, and she wonders how she has come to this—how she can hesitate for even a moment—how she has lost so much of herself that she doesn't even care about a young girl's life.

She takes a deep breath and dives into the water, back toward Annette, back toward the shore, straining to keep the child in sight beyond the swelling mounds of the ocean. The shifting gray sea shoves its wide shoulders against her.

STAY. STAY. STAY.

She kicks her legs and pummels her fists through the waves, hoping she will reach her in time. Her arms and legs are suddenly so heavy. Her body is becoming so difficult to move. She feels as if she's in a dream now, struggling in slow motion against the sea, thrashing through the water again and again, not sure if she is moving at all. Annette is bobbing up and down on the water—the waves are tossing her back and forth like a beach ball. Samantha kicks her legs harder, but the hands of the sea are holding her down by her ankles. Her lungs and heart are burning. She hopes she won't be too late. She hopes she will reach her in time. She can hear the seagull far above her, far above the roaring gray sea. She hopes the seagull is not the last sound that Annette is hearing—that she is not already dying.

STAY! STAY! STAY! the sea shouts in her ears.

Without warning, a pain blasts through her belly, as if her body is turning inside out and splitting in half, and the sea all around her is suddenly silent, inexplicably silent. Confused, she looks up at the gray sky. It's flapping silently above her. Why is everything so quiet? What can it mean? Before she can decide what it means, a giant wave begins turning her upside down in slow motion. A fat, wet pillow is covering her nose and mouth and pushing her down, farther and farther down, deep into the water, back to the place she used to be, long before she was born.

It would be easy now, she thinks, as she goes down. *Very easy.* She can die very quickly now; she can get away.

The sea is pulsing and gurgling in her ears. *STAY. STAY. STAY.* She follows the sound, letting herself sink farther and farther down.

It would be easy now, very easy.

But then, far away, far above her, she hears the muffled cry of the seagull, calling out again and again. She remembers Annette's distorted face in the water. When the seagull screams once more, far above her, Samantha lifts her arms through the water and reaches high above her head, far beyond the pain in her belly. She latches onto the sound of the seagull as if it's a rope, pulling her to the surface.

She cries out when she breaks through the watery membrane of the sea. She can hear the seagull calling again and again, just above her, and she can see Annette, a hundred feet away, bobbing lifelessly on the waves. She clings to the sound of the seagull above her and reaches out to Annette in slow motion. The sound of the seagull keeps urging her on, pulling her forward through the surging gray sea.

Annette's head has fallen to one side in the water, her neck limp, her mouth open, as if she is only resting on the arms of the sea. Samantha locks her elbow around the little girl's chin and strains to look beyond the waves. The eyes of the town are closed, blinded with shutters. One shutter of one house is banging in the wind, winking cynically at her again and again. Samantha closes her eyes and concentrates on the cry of the seagull above her, beyond the burning in her legs and belly. She wonders why the sea is becoming so silent again, why she can't hear it rising and falling all around her. Is this a dream? Did she drown long ago? Is she drowning again and again—has she been lost at sea forever? She kicks her legs harder at the sound of the seagull, while the ocean surges silently all around her.

She is surprised to hear the rush of the sea again when she stumbles out of the water, her hair clinging to her neck like long strands of seaweed. Annette's bony legs flop onto the sand as she lowers the child to the ground and places one ear against her chest. The little girl's heart is thumping wildly, like a trapped seagull batting against the hull of an overturned boat. Samantha presses her fingertips against her chest. With a convulsive shiver, the girl whimpers and coughs up a foaming gray stream of the sea. And then she opens her eyes and calmly smiles up at her, as if she has just awakened from a peaceful nap.

Samantha falls back onto the sand and stares up at the gray sky, gulping for air, staring at the wrinkled rag that has been hung out to dry. Her legs and arms are shaking and trembling, but the sand is solid against her back.

Annette reaches over and spreads her cold little fingers across Samantha's face. *Thanks*, the little girl whispers in English, directly into her ear.

The word swishes in her ear and then swishes out to sea. Samantha takes a deep breath, filling her lungs with the gray October air.

The seagull suddenly swoops down at her.

VIE! VIE! VIE! it calls.

Samantha watches it circle overhead, its white wings flashing like a mirror against the gray sky.

VIE! VIE! VIE! it calls again.

A single hot tear slides down her cheek as she listens to the familiar sound, as she listens to the sound she used to love so much, as she recognizes its meaning at last.

VIE! VIE! LIFE! LIFE! it calls again.

Samantha holds her breath and shields her face from the gray sky, and then she feels her first wave of hate for Stanley Wald sweeping over her, for what he did to her—for what she allowed him to do to the two little girls that had almost died today.

LIFE! LIFE! LIFE! the seagull calls. Samantha listens to the sound, circling above the pain in her belly. She wonders what the word for seagull is in Spanish, what the word sounds like when it sails across the wild October sea. She wonders if she can ever paint a single sound someday.

LIFE! LIFE! LIFE! the seagull calls again, and then it sails away from her, over the swelling waves of the gray October sea, its white wings flapping against the gray sky, heading, all alone, for the sandy shores of Spain.

Samantha clutches her stomach and turns over on her side, away from Annette, opening and closing her mouth in slow motion, trying to swallow the pain. And then, before she can stop it, the pain shrieks up from her belly, through her heart, ripping the very fabric of the sky. The sea jumps back and gasps, startled at the sound of a single soul splitting in two.

LIFE! LIFE! LIFE! the seagull calls again, and then it is gone, leaving her sobs far behind, heading, all alone, for the sandy shores of Spain.

A Time to be Born

Long before sunrise, La-Tu heard the first resonance of thunder, pulsing like a distant drumbeat, far beyond the village. Her heart quickened in response, even though she knew she was foolish to have any hope. It was too late for her—for them. She knew that. But something deep within her stirred, and she couldn't ignore the ancient feelings. *Maybe this time would be the time.*

The thunder pulsed again, closer than before. In a few moments it would begin its steady, determined march across the mountains. Nothing could stop it now. As the crimson feather tree outside the open window quivered in its sleep, La-Tu drew her woven blanket to one side and felt for her shoes in the darkness.

"You promised you wouldn't go."

La-Tu frowned and then slipped on her shoes in silence.

"La-Tu!"

"I didn't promise, Roonere," she said, louder than she had intended. "You're the one who said we'd stay home."

When he didn't answer, La-Tu sat on the edge of the bed and stared out the window, her hands folded in her lap. She was so weary of this conversation. They had been over it again and again during the long months of the last Dry Season. Through the lacy silhouette of the feather tree, she could see black clouds already circling the two moons, boiling higher with each new beat of thunder. The entire village was hushed, but she could feel the throb of anticipation. Everyone had been awake for hours, waiting. From a nearby house, she heard a suppressed whisper, followed by a stifled giggle.

She took a deep breath and turned to her husband. He was still lying on his back, shielding one side of his face with one arm. Two pools of moonlight had settled onto his jaw. His eyes were closed—his lips were set in a grim line. He looked so tired and old. When had his face become white and flaky? When had the youthful green luminescence of his skin faded away? The seasons had passed so quickly, leaving their youth far behind. What was she thinking? She was nothing but a foolish old woman.

When her gaze lingered upon him, Roonere finally opened his eyes and offered a slight smile. "I'll help you dress," he said finally, unable to control the emotion in his voice.

La-Tu blinked back her tears and nodded, just as the light from both moons suddenly dimmed, and a persistent roll of thunder vibrated the wall next to their bed. "We'll need to hurry," she whispered.

They dressed in silence. This was their fifth Rain Festival. When La-Tu draped the ceremonial robe over Roonere, with only the shifting beams of moonlight to guide her, she knew this Festival would be their last. Her hands hesitated on his stooped shoulders. How straight and tall—how muscular and strong—he had been in his youth, when she had dressed him for the first time, swelling with the love and hope of a new bride. It was so long ago. There had been so many disappointments—so many years of emptiness. When he turned to drape her own robe around her shoulders, she almost told him to stop. But then, thunder rumbled through the village again, vibrating the polished dirt floor beneath them. *This time could be the time.*

When they closed the door to their hut behind them, the path winding through the night was already filled with a long procession of villagers, heading sedately and silently to *The Place of Great Joy and Great Sorrow.* A family of seven ahead of them turned to them in surprise, but La-Tu took Roonere's hand and held her head high. She proceeded as proudly as she could, although she knew how old she must look, even in this muted light. She clutched the tiny Receiving Robe to her chest and avoided the pity in their eyes. Who were they to judge? Who were they to know, for certain? With their Creator, anything was possible. *This time could be the time.*

The Place of Great Joy and Great Sorrow was some distance from the village, near the base of the mountains. They hadn't walked far in the throbbing heat when La-Tu could feel Roonere losing his strength at her side. Discreetly gripping his hand more fiercely, she tried to support some of his weight. At one time he would have rebuked her silently with a wave of his hand. But this Festival was different. He was old now; he accepted her aid without complaint. Leaning on her shoulder, he felt light to her, as if a part of him had already left this world. La-Tu swallowed the lump in her throat. This would be the last time she would ever walk beside Roonere to *The Place of Great Joy and Great Sorrow*. When she came again, she would come alone, with only his coffin at her side.

Lightning suddenly branched across the sky, and the ground trembled beneath them as they paused to allow a wedding party to proceed in front of them. The bride, her green cheeks glowing with youth and anticipation, averted her eyes to avoid looking at La-Tu. La-Tu didn't reprimand the young woman, even in her heart. It had been five Rain Festivals—over fifty years—since her own wedding, but she remembered what it was like to be young. She knew exactly how the bride felt tonight, regal and proud in her wedding robe—filled with love and hope and optimism. Someday this bride might look back and regret her arrogant dismissal of a barren old woman. But tonight the girl didn't want to see a face weary with years of disappointment and emptiness; she didn't want to be reminded that there could be pain and suffering in the world.

    The bride's mother frowned at La-Tu. She thought she was going to speak to her, to scold her for casting an unlucky shadow on her daughter's Night of Joy. Instead, the mother merely hissed beneath her breath and then walked on, swelling her chest farther and farther out, as she held her end of the nuptial canopy higher and higher into the air. La-Tu took a deep breath. How different her own mother had been. Under similar circumstances, Mama would have smiled kindly at a barren old woman. But Mama was gone now—and Father—and Sister. La-Tu closed her eyes and concentrated on her footsteps, gripping Roonere's hand harder than before.

    She remembered the night that she and Roonere had first walked this very path over fifty years ago. She had been young and pretty then, although she had taken her youth and beauty for granted at the time. Roonere had been a handsome, imposing youth, walking proudly beside her, gently holding her slender hand against his barreled chest, close to his heart. Some grooms went to *The Place of Great Joy and Great Sorrow* with trepidation—even fear—but not Roonere. He had been strong and sure in those days, sure of his love for La-Tu, sure of the joy that would be theirs in the future. Father and Mama and Roonere's parents had held each corner of the nuptial canopy high into the air, proud of the young couple. Whenever La-Tu glanced at Mama, Mama would turn her head slightly, warning her not to speak, and then she would smile reassuringly out of the side of her mouth. La-Tu's sister had walked with a light step behind them, clutching a gold Receiving Robe to her chest. It had been La-Na's Third Rain Festival then, and she was still filled with hope. She wouldn't go home empty-handed this time. The last Festival had been an aberration, a fluke. It wouldn't be the same this time. When La-Tu turned to look at her, La-Na's eyes glowed with anticipation. As La-Tu thought of her sister now, she tried to remember her as she had been at that very moment on that night so long ago, energized by hope and loving anticipation, her lips forming a sweet smile, the golden scales around her face sparkling as electricity crackled in the air all around them. Two hours later, her sister's beautiful face was distorted with grief, already a macabre reflection of her former self. By the time the next Rain Festival arrived, La-Na was dead, the victim of a disease that had robbed her of her youth and beauty and had literally split her heart in two. The Healers had never understood its origin, but La-Tu did: Her sister's heart had begun breaking that night in *The Place of Great Joy and Great Sorrow*.

La-Tu gripped Roonere's hand more tightly. She wouldn't think of the past now. She wouldn't think of all the times she had walked down this path with Roonere before, clutching the Receiving Robe that she had woven during the first months of their marriage. She wouldn't think of all the years she had waited for their Second Rain Festival to begin, only to be devastated when the rain began pummeling the ground, turning the dry, packed soil to mud, while she and Roonere had stood waiting in the pouring rain, their shoulders hunched, desperately searching the ground in front of them for some sign of life.

A new reverberation of thunder and a sudden breath of wind pushed them forward, closer to their destination. *This time could be the time.*

La-Tu and Roonere filed into *The Place of Great Joy and Great Sorrow* behind the wedding party and quietly assumed their proper positions. In front of them, arranged neatly in a row, were the marked places of everyone they had ever loved— the places of Great Joy and Great Sorrow, those of the past, as well as those of the future.

La-Tu glanced at the white stones on her left. Father, Mama, Sister, and Roonere's parents were there, beneath the ground. Someday, at some distant Festival, they would emerge from the soil in Glorified Resurrected bodies. But that Festival was far away, far in the future, when all the Prophecies had been fulfilled. She and Roonere would be lying beside them in the ground by then, turning to dust. La-Tu felt Roonere grip her hand as she focused on the five green stones directly in front of them. These were the Places of Great Joy; she would never believe they were Places of Great Sorrow. She examined each stone, one by one, satisfied that nothing had disturbed them since the last Festival. Five polished stones, deeply embedded in the hard ground, glowed as brightly as they had when she and Roonere placed them there over fifty years ago, in the privacy of their wedding canopy. How proud they had been, when they had seen the fruit of their love—five of them!—so easily conceived and buried in the soil as the rain began to seep beneath the cloth walls of their tent.

Roonere cleared his throat and drew La-Tu closer to him. She leaned her head on his shoulder, just a little, and let her eyes wander to the three stones that her sister and brother-in-law had placed in the ground so many years ago. The stones were leaning to one side and had begun to whiten with age; the unborn children beneath them had never emerged. They had broken her sister's heart. They were as dead as the rest of her family.

Oh, Sister, how have we come to this?

La-Tu suppressed a moan as a vein of lightning pulsated across the expanse of the black sky and a low rumble of thunder muffled the priest's first words:

"To everything, Beloved, there is a Season: A Time to be Born... A Time to Die...."

La-Tu held onto Roonere's hand, seeking his strength. With his head bowed, he was beginning to sway under her weight. She quickly raised her head from his shoulder, remembering that he was old now, that he no longer had any strength to spare. She glanced at the wedding party assembled not far from her sister's stones. Everyone in the group, including the parents, seemed very young, glowing with the luminescence of youth. What was she doing here? Why had she forced Roonere to come? She was a foolish woman, a foolish *old* woman. She had no business here. This was only a Place of Great Sorrow for her now. Everyone she had ever loved was buried here, and the man beside her—her only love—would soon join them.

La-Tu stifled a sob and clutched the Receiving Robe and Roonere's hand to her chest, as the clouds around the moons began to spin more rapidly and a renewed grumble of thunder shifted the ground beneath them. She felt a raindrop hit the top of her shoe—or was it a tear? From herself? From Roonere? When she turned to look at her husband, the rain began to fall, hissing at first as it hit the hot dust in spots and then steaming in earnest as it broke loose from the sky. Everyone was silent for a few moments, while the rain fell harder and the Priest's prayers continued, but soon the high-pitched cries of the Newly Emerged Ones began, rippling through the crowd, cascading into shouts of joy and laughter. La-Tu could hear sighs from the Bride and Groom as they laid their first egg in their wedding tent and, far to her right, a dozen plots away, La-Tu saw a tiny newborn emerge from the soil, kicking and screaming and reaching for the arms of a young, proud father.

La-Tu and Roonere stood shoulder to shoulder, watching in silence as shafts of rain speared the ground in front of them, quickly turning the packed soil to mud. For a moment, just a moment, as the rain continued to fall and the thunder began to rattle the ground, La-Tu thought she saw a glistening movement beneath one of their stones. She squeezed Roonere's hand, but he merely shook his head, not meeting her eyes, and she knew it was hopeless. Nothing was there. Nothing would ever be there. She closed her eyes. The Priest's prayers could no longer be heard above the rain and laughter. But, from far away,

La-Tu could hear a woman's wrenching cries. She knew what it meant. Some other woman had begun her own desperate life of emptiness.

"Let's go home."

La-Tu nodded, almost unable to recognize Roonere's voice at her side. Sorrow and resignation had sapped all of his strength. Why had she done this to him? Why had she brought him here again? She felt for his hand in the rain. Together, hand in hand, they began to inch their way past the family stones, each step a struggle in the thick mud. La-Tu didn't look back at their stones—didn't look back at Father or Mama or Sister or at their five children who had never Emerged. She clung to Roonere's hand, trying to support him as they passed the three stones of her sister. He stumbled then, blinded by the rain—or perhaps by his tears. When she helped him to his feet, he was shaking. She shouldn't have brought him here.

"La-Tu!" he whispered hoarsely. His hand was growing colder in her own, but he abruptly pulled away from her, almost losing his balance again, pointing to the ground. La-Tu didn't look down. Her gaze was focused on his white face, streaked with rain and tears. How would she find the strength to get him home?

And then she heard it. It was the sound of something cracking somewhere near them—the sound of mud beginning to gurgle. She whirled around to look at their stones, but the dark mud which surrounded them was pockmarked with puddles of rain, as silent and as unforgiving as ever.

"Roonere?"

He wasn't looking at their stones. Instead, he was surging forward, searching the mud around the stones of her sister. There—just upon the surface, was a tiny bubble—and then another.

La-Tu strained to see over Roonere's shoulder. She leaned forward, desperately wiping the rain from her eyes. Something was emerging from the soil. It was a little face, the tiniest face, coated with mud, its eyes blinking in surprise. With a single sweep of his old hand, Roonere pulled it from the slippery mud, lifted it by its feet, and held it high in the air until its face turned bright green. It hung motionless for one long moment before it began to flail wildly in protest, screaming its first breath of air. Roonere turned to La-Tu, up-righting the newborn and gently cradling its head as he handed the child to her.

La-Tu couldn't move at first. Her wrinkled hands trembled as she took the little girl, who looked so much like La-Na, into her arms. When she wrapped the Receiving Robe around her, she buried her face into the baby's wet hair and took a deep breath. Her heart thumped an extra beat and then swelled with love at the newborn's fresh, sweet scent. All the years of loneliness and emptiness vanished, as if they had never existed. *This time was the time!*

At her side, Roonere was wrapping his arms around her and the child, holding them close. But, without warning, as the rain fell harder and the thunder and lightning threatened to topple the mountains around them, he began to shake again, more violently than before. Alarmed, La-Tu looked away from the baby to search her husband's contorted face.

For the first time in years, Roonere bared his teeth and threw back his head and began to laugh, loudly and robustly, as tears and rain streamed down his face. La-Tu clutched the child close to her chest and started to laugh too as Roonere suddenly lifted both her and the baby high into the air, high above his head and held them securely there, with all the strength of his love, in the warm, sacred rain.

The sound of the old couple's laughter echoed far above the thunder, far above the crowd. Everyone turned to see where it was coming from—this laughter that was so loud and joyful and strong—this laughter that had waited for a lifetime—this laughter that was booming high above the thunder, high above the mountains, heading for the two moons and the Heavens beyond. It was more powerful than any sound

which could be heard that night in *The Place of Great Joy and Great Sorrow.*
　This time was the time!

Brother Hop-a-long

If you see a bearded man on a street corner shrieking Russian proverbs while handing out *Snoopy for President* buttons and screaming at passing cars, "My God! You almost hit me," please let me know. If you see someone in tattered tennis shoes buying wilted vegetables at half-price in Los Angeles, or someone in bare feet reading Huckleberry Finn by the Mississippi River in Hannibal, Missouri, or someone in sandals simply hopping through the Phoenix Zoo with his shoulders raised and his head thrown back, please let me know: You've found my long-lost brother.

Richard's been missing for five years. During that time I've seen him once or twice and have received several collect phone calls from him. But I've never been able to write to him or to call him because he never furnishes addresses—they might fall into unscrupulous hands—and he's never had a telephone installed—the cost is too exorbitant.

Last year he showed up at our farm, but no one in the family got to see him. We were in the barn milking, and when we came up to the house, we found a hastily scribbled note:

Sorry I missed you. Let's try to get together in

five years. Best Regards, etc., Richard

Two years ago I had his location pinned down: I had the telephone number of the parking lot of the grocery store where his girlfriend's grandmother did her weekly shopping.

"Richard's a fine boy," she said, when I caught her passing one Saturday afternoon. "So considerate, polite, and giggly. Tell me—what's he do for a living?"

"He must be working for the Mob," Mom sighed a few weeks ago.

"No," Dad answered. "His hopping would be too conspicuous."

From $5 a day working in the cotton fields of Arkansas to $300 a day working for an electronics company in New York, Richard has always deplored labor. "It's disgusting, degrading, despicable," he says, as he tosses his hair back with his fingers and grins, jutting his lower jaw out of alignment and fluttering his long, blond eyelashes. "I was meant for greater things."

Richard discovered he was meant for greater things when he was a freshman in high school. At that time, he was seriously considering the idea of quitting school and becoming a bum. But then something happened: Richard was saved—he "found" Dostoevsky. No one is sure of the details. Some speculate that he met someone who showed him the Way; others claim he saw the Master Himself. One day he was reading comic books;

the next day he was reading *Crime and Punishment*. Instead of becoming a bum when he was fourteen, Richard went on to graduate from high school and college and *then* became a bum.

But he's not a total bum. He works a few months a year and spends the rest of his time collecting unemployment checks, dreaming about the beaches in California, and reminiscing about the summer of '68 when he and a friend toured the coast in a '52 Kaiser. As soon as the Kaiser is mentioned, Richard whips out one of his diaries and reads silently to himself, chewing his fingernails and giggling and snorting every few seconds. His favorite story of the trip concerns the time he and his friend were stopped by a state trooper on a freeway in California. The trooper carefully explained that they had to go more than 10 miles per hour on a super highway. After being told to get rid of the junker, Richard coasted off the freeway and abandoned the old Kaiser near the ocean.

"I like to think that the '52 Kaiser is part of the sea now," Richard reflects in one of his quiet moments. "That should be one of the deeper themes of My Novel."

Richard has been working on His Novel for half of his life—since he was thirteen years old. He also has many volumes of diaries that date back to his early childhood. When he was living at home, the journals lined one wall of his room. I would often gaze at them and wonder what marvels they contained. But they were Private. *Authorized Personnel Only!* was the sign above the bookcase. Richard has always been a suspicious person and would sometimes openly accuse me of reading his diaries, saying that a speck of dust that he had scientifically positioned on page 183 had move 1.52 centimeters. I would cry, declaring my innocence. After a time, Richard would forgive me. "Go get me some pop and potato chips and we'll forget about it this time," he would say nobly.

In addition to being noble, Richard has always been brave. Once, when we lived in the city, a gang of teenaged vigilantes came to our house to find the rascal who had been slitting bicycle tires at school. Richard quickly bolted the doors and took me into a back room and hid me in a closet.

"Don't worry, I'll take care of this," he said, as he quickly disappeared from sight. While I trembled in the closet, I could hear distant booing and rocks bombarding the roof of our house. After a time, the mob drifted away. When I finally peeked out through the closet door, my brave brother opened the hatch in the ceiling of the hallway and hopped down from the attic.

As well as being noble and brave, Richard has always been kind-hearted. In our neighborhood there was a boy who thought he was a Martian.

Naturally, everyone on our block made fun of him. When Richard heard me laughing at the boy one day, he grabbed me by the elbow and rushed me into the house.

"For shame, for shame, little sister. Think of that poor, lonely boy alone in his room every day, flying around in a make-believe spaceship. No one likes him. No one wants him. What kind of a person are you—to be so cold, so cruel, so thoughtless?" When I started to cry, Richard said, "I'm sure the little Martian will forgive you this time if you go and get me some pop and potato chips." He hopped off to his room and waited for his snack.

One day, when he was 21 years old, Richard hopped out of the house with his suitcase filled with diaries, manuscripts, pop, and potato chips and became my long-lost brother. I saw him two years ago, and we talked like we did in the old days:

He said that work is disgusting, degrading and despicable, that he was meant for greater things. He fondly recalled his trip in '68 with the '52 Kaiser. He once again accused me of his reading his diaries and reminded me that I should never have made fun of the little Martian boy. With a smug smile, he reported that His Novel was almost completed. When I told him I've finished Mine, he pounded his fist on the coffee table.

"Impossible!" he yelled. He then puckered out his lower lip, rolled back his eyes, and jumped up into the air, giggling as he began hopping up and down. A moment later, he stopped and put one arm around my shoulders. "Listen, little sister," he said in a low, subdued voice, "I'll forgive you for stealing My Novel if you go and get me some pop and potato chips."

As I hopped off to the kitchen, Richard crossed himself and thanked Dostoevsky that I turned out okay.

Haiku

Author's Note

The haiku in this section were written over a period of four decades, beginning when I was a mere "child" and continuing into the present. Many of them were published during the 1980s and 1990s in haiku journals such as *Modern Haiku, Frogpond, Brussels Sprout, and Cicada.* One or two appeared in *Haiku Quarterly (USA)*, which I myself edited for several years in the early 1990s. Since most of these haiku were never intended to be read in any particular order, they have been separated by generous portions of "white space" so that each haiku can be considered for what it is—an independent moment in time. To give the collection some sense of order, the haiku have been grouped by seasons, even though that arrangement is often arbitrary.

I've been somewhat hesitant to offer a collection of haiku at all. Oddly enough, although I've been writing haiku since I was a child, I don't consider myself to be a haiku poet. I usually write novels and short stories—not poetry. The haiku in this book are merely fleeting moments of time that I've tried to capture as I've lived my life. They are certainly no better—and possibly no worse—than millions of haiku which have undoubtedly been scribbled on scraps of paper throughout the centuries, even before haiku was recognized as a form of Japanese poetry. (I must add here that my native language is English, and my haiku have sprouted from a well-established American branch of haiku writing. Even so, some haiku in this collection may "stray" at times from accepted American standards and traditions.)

I decided to proceed with this collection *not* because I think of myself as a "great" haiku poet but because a part of my writing life has been so scattered throughout the years—on snippets of paper and in various haiku magazines. I wish that everyone who has ever written haiku—or any type of poetry—had the time to collect his or her favorite poems into a book. Not many of us will be called gifted poets, but our offerings as a whole reflect who we are—an ephemeral embodiment of humanity, here on earth for an amazingly brief moment of time. It is our duty to try to preserve our creative expressions, no matter how humble they may be.

In that spirit, I dedicate these haiku not only to my husband, my family, and my friends—but also to everyone—in the past, present, and future—who has ever attempted to capture a few moments in time before they're gone forever.

~ Lynda Eymann

Lynda Eymann

racing the moon
from pole to pole
the long empty highway

Spring

morning chill
the wisteria shivers
lavender snowflakes

Lynda Eymann

seeds through her fingers
a flicker of finches
from every tree

after the cat's death
the silent ray of sunlight
at my feet

Lynda Eymann

after the cat's death
a lilt in
the mourning dove's call

web in the fence
                    stretching out
the March wind

Lynda Eymann

again she checks
all the locked windows
lilac in the wind

to dust,
the sparrows swirl within
the whip's sound

the cross-darkened sun
the sudden weight
of his last breath

the empty tomb
the sparrow peers within
the wing's sound

Lynda Eymann

in the blue crevice
between rooftops
cathedral bells

Summer

Lynda Eymann

Praying for Crows

almost home
almost smelling
the Mississippi

zigzagging straight down
to the Mississippi River
grandma's brick street

in grandma's bed
floating on goose feathers
her Irish brogue

the lapping water
the bed sinks deeper this year
grandma mama me

in murky night
riverboats passing
in murky night

the riverboat tugs
the pit in my belly—
you used to be six?

ninety-year-old sigh
'twas no time at'all, darlin'
no time at'all

Lynda Eymann

after the heat
of the cotton field
crawdads in the creek

shaded creek
knee deep
in trees

Lynda Eymann

deep into the roots
of the gnarled oak
the minnow's path

the old home site
a copperhead curled around
a broken mirror

Lynda Eymann

down the cellar steps
August sun on my back
my shadow shivers

Praying for Crows

dinner bell
shadows of catfish
lost in the willows

Lynda Eymann

dusk
the damp mare plows
her last shadow

dinner bell
the darting shadows
of freed minnows

Lynda Eymann

dusk
in my hands
new potatoes

Praying for Crows

moonless homecoming
a fruit jar of fireflies
on the back porch step

Lynda Eymann

the screen door closes
night enters
the plowed field

Praying for Crows

last of the air
caught in the curtains
last of the light

Lynda Eymann

night without breath
heat lightning ripples
the hot tin roof

locusts
the madness in
her hair

Lynda Eymann

a dream of rain
sand pitting
all the windows

frogs
their song circles
the brightest moon

Lynda Eymann

last night of summer
a falling star scatters
the frogs

Autumn

watercolored
the sun rises
in rain

Lynda Eymann

upon each hill
half of a clapboard house
in autumn mist

abandoned park
carousel horses riding
the wind

Lynda Eymann

no one knows her name
windblown cicada shells
piled at her door

Praying for Crows

through the gaping holes
of the abandoned birdhouse
the whistling wind

Lynda Eymann

dreamless night
the full moon bounces
from branch to branch

Castle Chillon

after night's rain
between the cooing of doves
his steady breath

huddled in downpour
gulls shift legs, then eyes at
passing umbrellas

descending in night
slick steps to street below
smell of rain on stone

midnight rain pelting
her black umbrella
the train's long hiss

at Castle Chillon
the train's last whistle
catches her breath

after night's rain
mist rising from the lake
his scent leaving the sheets

Lynda Eymann

full moon
my kite chases
a bat

moonlit steam
a toe at a time
into the old tin tub

Lynda Eymann

crescent moon
above the eagle's nest
a curve in the wind

Winter

the mountain
in fog
in goat bells

Lynda Eymann

down the mountain path
the goats tilt their horns
into sleet

in the wolf's track
the pink tip
of my goat's ear

Lynda Eymann

moonless night
the newest lamb
motherless

roof of winter stars
the slow breathing
of goats dreaming

Lynda Eymann

the longest winter—
a stillborn goat
with long white hair

Praying for Crows

tail-lights in snow
waving waving goodbye
my father's hat

Lynda Eymann

deep in quilts
rain and sleet
on a distant roof

Praying for Crows

a last flutter
from the henhouse
falling snow

Childhood Poems

Lynda Eymann

Christmas Day
(age: 7)

Christmas Day is a holiday,
I will sing hurray on Christmas Day
I will open my presents
I will be so gay
On Christmas Day.

I'll be happy
I'll be gay
I always am on Christmas Day.

Not Self-Conscious?
(age: 11)

Do I look all right when I walk down a street,
Am I making a pig of myself when I eat,
Is my slip showing when I rise from a chair,
Are people watching me or don't they care,
Am I too ugly or too pretty,
Do people regard me with envy or pity,
Am I too skinny or too tall,
Are my feet too big or too small,
Is my posture too straight or am I "all bent over,"
Do I act too silly or too sober,
Are my clothes too plain or are they too plush?
Oh, no—I'm not self-conscious!

Doodling
(age: 11)

Doodling requires no training at all.
Get something to doodle on—a paper or wall.
While you're doodling, think of this ancient art.
How do you think cavemen discovered that first spark?
And what about Columbus? He was doodling one day
Looking for the Indies, he found America's Way.
Originally Leonardo da Vinci was painting a poodle,
But someone broke in one night and started to doodle.

So doodle faithfully, my friend, each day,
Don't get discouraged, for doodling will pay.

Mammy
(age: 12)

Mammy, yea is my puddin' pie
An' that ain't no lie,
Yea goes to work every mornin' at 7 o'clock,
An' yea don't get home till it's near'y dark,
Yea makes a livin' for a family, a troublesome one,
Yea ain't never had eny fun,
So sits yearself down in a cheer,
Remember I loves yea, Mammy dear.

On Saturday yea fixes the house nice 'n purty,
But durin' the week it gets awfully durty,
At 9 o'clock yea comes and tucks me in tight,
Yea says, "Say your prayers," and kisses me good night.

So sit yeaself down somewhere.
Remember I is your daughter, and I do care!

Violet Hill
(age: 14)

The willows by the creek sway in the breeze
Along with the violets
beneath the trees.

Nearby, a house stands on a hill
Ragged and Forlorn,
silent and still.

A grave behind a church awaits a child
That disturbs no more
The flowers growing wild.

A mother's hope is
Borne with grace
To its final resting place.

A father's mind cannot understand
The stilling of his helping hand.

The willows wail with the Mourners' cry
The violets add their feeble sigh.

They will heal the earth
That was parted
To cradle the life that only started.

Lynda Eymann

Black Man
April 12, 1969 (age: 15)

No more marching,
Plight or preaching,
War or worry,
Tears or teaching.
No more starving,
Hate or hearing,
Lies of living,
Fate or fearing.
No more searching,
Care or caring,
Guilt or grieving,
Death or daring.

Some six feet down
In earthen cast—
And solid ground
I'm free at last!

*Author's note:
I wrote this for Martin Luther King
a year after his death*

The Ship Arrives
November 1970 (age: 16)

Ah, I see the ship!
So long it's been at sea searching for me
And I've waited as custom deems
Yet here I sit so quiet and still,
I, a prisoner for many waves in this tower,
Stolen as a child by some ungodly power.

What prince has come to my rescue?
Or perhaps a craftsman to tune my lute?
A king would be nice with gifts and things
Or perhaps a pirate to steal me away
To isles of coconuts and salty waves.
But a king brings balls and so many rites,
And a pirate brings babes and womanly trite.
But a craftsman would be nice.

Or perhaps this ship is only passing
And will leave me as before—alone with my lute
And the stuffed parrot above me.

Yes, I'm sure the ship is passing;
if I sit very still it shall surely pass in peace.
And then I'll tune my lute myself,
and it will sing me to sleep,
now as before and forever more.

Lynda Eymann

If You've Ever—
April 1971 (age: 17)

If you've ever had your very own tree and your
very own swing,
and charged people only a puppy a ride, you'd feel
pretty proud—
even if you got only one customer.
If you've ever watched your brave puppy shake a
snake to death before your very own eyes,
and two weeks later see him do the same to your
kitty,
you'd feel pretty sick—
even if your puppy shrank in shame at your feet.

If you've ever run from a big brother dressed up as
a bear,
And shrieked so loud that it surprised even you,
you'd feel pretty proud—
even if you couldn't breathe when you fell over the
hidden wire.
If you've ever mocked the way the fat Simmons'
twins chewed gum
and chomped away before their very own eyes
and one whacked you across the face,
you'd feel pretty sick—
even if your big brother's best friend beat up that
fat Simmons' twin for you.

Praying for Crows

If you've ever gone with your dad everywhere,
following him up and down the hills and helping him call in the cows,
you'd feel pretty proud—
even if you got lost in the sage grass.
If you've ever shivered around an empty wood stove
and bonked your head on a creek full of ice
and watched your dad drive away on Christmas morning,
never to come back,
you'd feel pretty sick—
even if you had a thousand Christmas gifts left to open.

My Aunt's Confession
November 1970 (age: 16)

Maybe it wasn't so long ago
or so far away
that I knew everything
there was to say.

Starched dresses
and curly hair
red lipstick
and perfumed stares.

I knew everything
there was to say
in by-gone plays.

But, now, somehow,
I can't tell
whether the sun
is setting
or rising.

I guess it could be
either
or neither
for me.

Francisco, the Wandering Guitarist
July 19, 1971 (age: 17)

He gave the veils and clicking heels to me
And lazy villas filled with summer sighs.
The lights of candle love became as free
As summer wine, as old as vineyard skies.
Without a sound the sun went weeping down
And crashed upon a mountain side, as he
Released his love and soul to us with brown
And earthen warmth. A flying, childish glee
Embraced my soul, and I desired to leave
My faded jeans and television shows
For sweeping skirts, fiesta fires—to weave
Francisco's soul with mine. Francisco goes
From night to night and woods to town to bring
A candle's flame to little girls in spring.

Lynda Eymann

Brother In Memoriam

flower child then

golden hair
halo hair
no one spared

flower child then

supper war
nightly war
pass some more

flower child then

birthday pick
chosen quick
brother sick

flower child then

severed hair
sailing there
brother scared

flower child then
golden gone
rolling on

brother where?

Long gone
Ever gone.
Never spared.

Flower child then
I remember when

Praying for Crows

Vietnam '72
(age: 18)

The morning mist
rose
like hickory smoke,
soft and slow,
and shadows on the ground
floated like down
in circles
and silence

in and out tracing
about facing

circling walls
circling drills

the circling moon stands still

Moon White,
Moon White,
How many'll die tonight?

Lynda Eymann

For Norma Jean
(age: 19)

Let me hold your doll, Norma Jean
Let me hold her while you sleep
She's lacy white and warm
Promise I promise
I'll give her back
I need her now as you needed
her then:
The wind's blowing again.
I don't want to sleep like
You, Norma Jean
Your silence I can't understand
So just let me hold
Her for a lullaby
The wind's blowing and
It's too early for bed.

One Summer Night

If I could return to that summer's eve
Would I still fly with you across the night?
Or would I stop this time and safely leave
Your shadow alone in the moon-flecked light?
Would I dare recall my love from flight?
Would I move aside when you reached to part
The wide-eyed stars and love holding tight
To the folded wings of my raptured heart?
Or would I repeat the past with no dart
Of doubt, slipping again from Father's house,
Caught in your promises, our journey's start,
Caught in my love for you, my future spouse?
How bold of you to love me forever
When that one night was the same as never.

Lynda Eymann

Lost

crisscrossing the woods
calling her name
my goat is missing

even in daylight
on a nearby hill
coyotes yapping

down by the creek
Father raises his hand
don't come near

glimpsing only hooves
in the cave of her belly
her unborn kids

the long walk home
following Father's shoes
shadows of vulture wings

Nanny Goat

Do you remember Nanny Goat?
How she would wait for spring?
She'd grunt and groan and yawn and nod--
A toady-tummied thing.
With puppy-woods a'bloomin' then,
You'd hold and stroke her nose,
And sun and bugs a'hummin' loud,
Her lizard eyes would close.

When womb-mates punched her in and out,
She'd grunt and groan and sigh,
She'd smell the grass, she'd smell the air
And lick the triplets dry.
They'd grunt and groan and yawn and nod--
You'd hold and stroke each nose,
With sun and bugs a'hummin' loud,
All lizard eyes would close.

(In Memory of Toggie)

Lynda Eymann

Winter Came Last Night

Winter came last night
quietly in the night

The pond lured the snowflakes
and froze them as they fell
they sleep in the ice
like big white moths
mummied in a web

Winter came last night
quietly in the night

the dogs stiffen their tails and rigidly watch
as I throw a rock and then another—
they fly through the air making promises,
they fly through the air believing,
they hit with a hollow thud and bounce away,
defeated.
You can't chip the ice around a frozen pond's
heart.

Winter came last night
quietly in the night

The hill has grown its antlers,
tall and black, bare and still,

Praying for Crows

peering down,
not daring to blink,
the herd of them
pretending
to be trees again,
they stand ready to scatter over the cold-white
hills,
dragging the dogs with them,
dragging their panting-red tongues and frosted-
black fur after them,
leaving just the winter to watch

The dogs watch me still

They twist their heads
they lock their ears
they wonder what I see
I wonder what they hear

I throw another rock
it thuds against my heart

Winter came last night
quietly in the night

It watches me still

About the Author:

Lynda Eymann has worked as an editor, quilt artist, and midwife (to goats). When she's not writing, she enjoys reading, quilting, knitting, and being with her husband and family.

Books by Lynda Eymann:

The Reluctant Time Traveler
Lord Justin Sittwell Claims a Wife
Before They're Gone Forever
Praying for Crows

Made in the USA
Columbia, SC
04 January 2025